Tales From Sri Lanka and India

Revathi Raj Iyer

Ukiyoto Publishing

All global publishing rights are held by

Ukiyoto Publishing

Published in 2022

Content Copyright © Revathi Raj Iyer
ISBN 9789360163419

*All rights reserved.
No part of this publication may be reproduced, transmitted, or stored in a retrieval system, in any form by any means, electronic, mechanical, photocopying, recording or otherwise, without the prior permission of the publisher.*

The moral rights of the authors have been asserted.

*This is a work of fiction. Names, characters, businesses, places, events, locales, and incidents are either the products of the author's imagination or used in a fictitious manner. Any resemblance to actual persons, living or dead, or actual events is purely coincidental.
This book is sold subject to the condition that it shall not by way of trade or otherwise, be lent, resold, hired out or otherwise circulated, without the publisher's prior consent, in any form of binding or cover other than that in which it is published.*

Enthralling mystery stories laced with love, passion, taboo, cultural snippets and above all, a spectacular climax!

J. Sam Daniel Stalin
Bureau Chief at NDTV, Chennai

In loving memory of my mother and father

Acknowledgements

A chance meeting with the renowned author, Mr. Ruskin Bond, during a staycation at Mussoorie.
A casual chat with the taxi driver whose ancestors were from the Balti community.
The monk at the temple in Christchurch, New Zealand, from whom I learnt meditation.
My family for their love and support.
Reviewers and book lovers who have appreciated both my books: "My Friendship with Yoga," and "Syra's Secret-Diverse Short Stories."
Mr. J Sam Daniel Stalin, Bureau Chief at NDTV, Chennai, for his blurb.

Heartfelt thanks to each one of you!

My gratitude to the divine Creator, for leading and guiding me in the path of creativity.

Contents

The Monk	1
A Mussoorie Tale	15
Glossary	33
About the Author	34

The Monk

I was ordained for monkhood right from the time I was born.

"Who made that decision? When? Why me?"

I was not even in the picture when the decision about my life was made. I believe that my destiny in this life was probably decided in my previous life by strange, unknown forces. I would never find the truth behind all this, but that did not change the fact that I was born to embrace monkhood.

The whole village was jubilant on my birth. Those days a baby was born not just in the family, but to the entire village. "It takes a whole village to raise a baby," is a popular saying that owes its beginnings to the good old times.

Coming back to my story: I came out of my mother's womb not knowing about my destiny, but my parents seemed to be well aware of it because they were fully prepared to forsake me at the tender age of six.

"Six years! Bloody hell, can you believe that?"

Apparently, this happens in Asian countries in sects that are guided by religious norms. I was born in Sri

Lanka, which made it holier. Here, the people believed that if a child was given away to monkhood, the whole generation in the family would be blessed. But if the mother was alive to witness her son in the robes of a monk, seven generations down the line would be blessed.

The villagers whispered that I was born to bless seven generations. To them, I was a reincarnation of God. I was predestined to lead a life of discipline and follow the rules and dictum of the holy transition, which I was not supposed to break.

"How could I break a discipline when I had no idea what indiscipline was all about?"

My parents nurtured me until I turned six. On my birthday, an event was held for a special prayer to invoke the Gods. This was led by a few bald men in saffron robes. I heard the word "monk" for the first time in my life. Somebody told me that they belonged to the monastery. I heard the word "monastery" for the first time too.

An elaborate feast was prepared by the women-folk and all the villagers ate at my house. The monks from the monastery were fed first along with the Head Priest.

Strangely, I recall this occasion as it was a turning point in my life. I remember holding the hand of an old monk as I walked away empty-handed from my house, my parents, my childhood, my pets and my village—the place of my birth. Familiarity faded away as I moved on, not knowing what life had in store for a little boy of six. The sun had set as usual, but its light shone brighter and prevailed for a very long time.

At that moment, I was born again.

******

We reached the monastery at night, after what seemed to be a very long drive through an unknown, rugged path. We were stopped in-between by men, with a long instrument. They checked our vehicle, then smiled, bowed to the monks and let us pass. I did not know who they were but would know much later that they were army men with guns, and the place we were stopped was a check-post. It was the period when there was strife between the Sinhalese and Tamil Tigers, who wanted to carve a portion of the country as an independent home—*Illam* of the Tamils.

After that incident, I must have fallen asleep until our destination. I was then led to my room by the same old monk whose hand I was holding as I left my village. The room was tiny, cold, and had a bed, closet and bookshelf. The toilet and bathrooms at the end of the corridor were meant to be shared by all those who lived on the same floor. I presume that I must have slept like a rock that night, overcome by sheer exhaustion.

I was neither frightened nor lonely, and for reasons unknown to me, I did not miss my parents. It was as if I had let go of them as well. However, I did miss the warmth of my bed, my pets and playmates—a coop full of little chicks and bunnies. I missed them all, dearly.

The next morning, I was woken up and led downstairs where all the monks were seated around a large table for breakfast. One of them made me sit on his lap. I ate a lot, much to the amazement of all the monks who were nibbling at their food. They reminded me of my chicks who would peck at the grains. I suppressed a smile.

What happened after that hearty meal was scary, indeed! I remember my shameful screams to this day.

I saw a dark, puny man with shabby clothes waiting for me in the courtyard. The old monk held my hand and we walked towards him. The monk told the puny man something in Sinhalese which I did not understand. I only knew bits of Tamil. My language and communication skills were very poor. In those times, village-folk went to school at any age they pleased and some did not even bother to. My parents did not send me to school, so I had not learnt to read or write.

Coming back to that unforgettable day of my life— the puny man nodded and opened a small, dirty box and pulled out a sharp knife that was gleaming. He forced me down and forbade me to move. I sat still, unable to take my eyes away from the knife. As he started toying with my head and hair, I felt a sharp pain. To my utter horror, I saw my shredded hair all around and over me. I wailed loudly and tried to get up and run, but two strong arms pinned me down. I wept; the tears would not stop. The job was done, I was tonsured and the puny man collected some coins and left.

Still in tears, I was taken to the shower in the courtyard where I was given a bath with a strong smelling powder and I emerged feeling drained of emotions. I felt numb. That is all I remember.

Thereafter, life at the monastery was much disciplined with lessons in English, Sinhalese, Scriptures, Prayer and Meditation. Each day ended by thanking God and seeking his forgiveness. I was a meek lad following it religiously, until all this grew on me and in all innocence, I embraced monk-hood. I was the youngest monk whom everybody revered, as if I was a being of rare sorts with magical prowess.

******

Today, as I lie in my bed at the monastery waiting to breathe my last, leave this body and emancipate my soul, I pray that the Almighty will understand and forgive me.

******

Some of you may have heard the story of how a petty thief reformed and became the famous sage Valmiki who wrote one of the greatest Indian epics, *Ramayana*. But imagine the same story backwards. It feels so wrong. This happened to me. I did not turn into a thief exactly, but I went against the rules of the monastery which a monk would never have dreamt of, but I dared to.

"Why?" Because thus far, my life was at the mercy of everybody but now I wanted to take charge and live it all up, just once. For twenty-five years of my life at the monastery, I knew nothing beyond the confines of its four walls. It was a very stringent life. I had read about Siddhartha, the ultimate Buddha. He was a prince who opted to be a monk. I had no such privileges or options. After all these years, I was filled with a sudden urge to experience life, be it a princely one or that of the so-called ordinary man. I wanted to escape from the monastery and this esteemed position before I was further elevated to a higher Order.

"What is wrong with that?" I had no one to ask. I didn't have the courage to seek advice, because I would be shunned and given even more rigorous training, as if twenty-five years were not enough!

However, all this changed to my advantage one day, when a businessman sought private audience with me. I noticed that he was old, stocky and spoke with a lisp.

"I have done the worst forms of crime. I have cheated. Still I have plenty of money and the going is good. But I have no mental peace. Please help me in restoring inner peace. I have come all the way from another country when I heard about you," he said.

"You look so peaceful and serene," he added and looked at me fixedly. Then he lowered his eyes as if trying to hide an expression—a fondness perhaps?

I pondered over his question and closed my eyes.

I had no idea about my global popularity. I was awestruck by this reality and the old man who had travelled miles to seek peace. *"But, was he aware that I too had a conflict in my mind? That my emotions were untapped and I felt caged and yearned to be set free, in order to explore my innermost desires and emotions?"*

It was highly ironic. Here was a person seeking my help, when in fact, I required help from somebody. I was in a dilemma. We sat in silence for some time and then I made up my mind.

"You have been doing all sorts of bad things in life. Can you do one more, as a favour to me?" I asked him.

He certainly had not bargained for this. His eyes widened with curiosity and then fear set in. I smiled at him as a way of reassurance. "Please do not be afraid, my dear friend. No harm will befall you. Listen carefully to me," I said.

The stranger sat in rapt attention waiting to hear my next words; it was going to hit him like a thunderbolt.

"I am asking you to kidnap me, take me somewhere far away from this monastery and expose me to a life of passion, love and pain. Teach me anything but it has to be a wonderful experience. In return, I will guide you to cope up with life and impart my teachings. I will give it all away to you."

The businessman looked at me in disbelief. He was quiet for a few minutes. Then he smiled strangely, as if he understood my mind and knew his course of action.

"How will I kidnap you?" he asked guardedly.

"That is your problem," I said. I had no clue how people got kidnapped. I lived in a secluded world of my own.

"We have a deal," saying this, he left.

I stared at his stocky figure until he vanished from sight and slowly from my mind.

******

A few days later, one night, I was woken up by a man. I could not see him as he wore a mask.

"I am going to kidnap you," he whispered in my ears.

"Okay, please do it then." I said calmly.

He rubbed something against my nose and a pungent odour filled my nostrils. I felt as if I was lifted by somebody. I was delirious.

"Was it my mother holding me in my arms?"

I then felt a jerky motion.

"Was I in a car or a cot that rocked?"

After what seemed like a lifetime of being unconscious, semiconscious and back to being unconscious, I finally woke up to unfamiliar surroundings in a cosy, warm bed. I got out of bed and surprisingly felt energetic. I was astonished to find myself in a very beautiful house, palatial with heavy golden drapes, chandeliers, carved pillars and large windows. The mansion was skirted by a garden with exotic flowers and fruits, lily pond and floral swings.

This was paradise for me but I was not alone. I saw a bevy of beautiful girls clad in minimum clothing, smiling and waving at me. They had long tresses with flower bands around their forehead and wore ornaments. One of them came closer to me and asked if I needed anything. I felt a rush of desire, and my body convulsed with mixed emotions that I never knew existed.

I gaped, not knowing what to say. My throat was dry and I asked for a glass of water. She giggled and handed me one. It tasted odd, sweet, sour and tangy. The water here was so different. But I liked it. I asked for more and more, to the point where I could hardly get up and felt unstable.

"Did water have such an effect in this palace?" I wondered. I was happy and sad and tears started coming out of my eyes. I blurted out my *mantras* and they were so slurred that I felt my tongue drag out each and every syllable. I was very hungry. I asked for food and ate everything that was served to me. I did not know what

I ate, but they were all very delicious. By then it was nightfall. I was wide awake. I could not see the businessman anywhere.

One of the most beautiful maidens came up to me and started playing with my body. I then knew what ecstasy was! I had never felt this way as a little boy, when my mother would bathe or clothe me. This was something different.

Every day it was the same routine; I drank, ate and played with the girls. The girls changed and I started enjoying myself.

Then one day, I was suddenly deprived of all this. No food, no drink, not even water, and no beautiful girls. With every passing hour I waited impatiently for the pampering to start, but nothing happened. I was hungry, thirsty and craved for love. That day, I learnt what heartache was.

The next day, the businessman came up to me and asked if my wish was fulfilled. I was furious when I saw him and demanded to know why I was treated badly the previous day.

"Isn't that what you wanted me to teach you? Both pleasure and pain?" he asked. It felt as if he was mocking me.

"Yes," I mumbled.

He then asked if I could keep my part of the deal.

"What in the name of God had I promised?" To my utter dismay and disbelief, I could not remember anything at all. My past was erased from my memory, as if a part of me was snatched away.

"What was the deal?" I asked after taking a few deep breaths.

The old man was now clearly frustrated and filled with rage, at my inability to keep up my word, whatever that was. He was a businessman, after all. He threatened to expose me and said he could even kill me.

That night, sleep eluded me. Even if he killed and dumped my body, who was going to miss me? It was best that he killed me. But he didn't do it. He said with some modesty that he was not unscrupulous. Kidnapping was as far as he would go, and even that he had done only at my behest.

"I do not want to have your blood on my hands. I shall not kill you. I will take you back to the monastery in the same manner I brought you here," he said.

I agreed. The process was repeated and I found myself in the monastery, in my room where the robe of a monk was neatly laid out. Back in familiar surroundings, I regained my memory; it all came back to me in a flash.

******

The next morning, as I came out of my room, everybody in the temple was astonished. Their eyes bore a look of admiration as they bowed and slowly walked away. I did not understand the reason for this strange look of respect at a person who had sinned. I had practically forgotten my life as a monk.

I was ashamed when I found out the truth behind this heightened level of reverence and adulation. They were under the impression that I had forfeited food, water and meditated in solitude, day and night for several days and had finally emerged out of the room like Buddha, with a light shining above my head.

No wonder they treated me differently now; with adoration and love, as if I was God. I had moved up in the Order. I decided to observe silence, my best recourse under the circumstances. But deep down, I knew that I had committed a wrong deed. I was guilt-ridden and felt burdened with the respect and love I was being showered with. I did not deserve it. This pained me, until one day I mustered the courage to confess. It had to be somebody who would listen to me with an open mind, without judging me.

I decided to wait. I waited and waited in silence, for a very long time.

Finally, one day, a young monk came to see me. There was something about him that brought back flashes of my childhood memories as a six-year-old boy. I was seeing myself in him, but he was pure and had not sinned. I knew he was the one I had been waiting for all these years. My calling had come. I had to confess or I couldn't be liberated.

I started talking to him. I told him everything.

The young monk heard me patiently and said, "You have not sinned."

I did not understand.

The young monk smiled kindly. He explained, "All that was *maya*, an illusion which played up your senses. The businessman got you kidnapped and kept you safe in one of his lovely mansions and you were looked after well. But he was shrewd. He had merely drugged you but made sure you were not overdosed. He even arranged medical check-ups. He knew your inner mind would transport you to that mansion of illusions that was tormenting you. You have been avenged by *maya* that momentarily snatched away your memories of the life you led as a monk. You have blessed many souls and continued your life as a monk at the monastery till your end. Thereby, you have also earned your reprieve."

I looked at the wise monk. I had one last question.

"Can you please explain how I kept my part of the promise to the businessman?" I asked.

The young monk continued, "That businessman was none other than your grandfather who had sworn to never set eyes on you when he got to know about your ordainment. He was the only person in the village who opposed the idea but it fell on deaf ears. So he left the village and since then has not been heard of. Destiny brought him here and when he saw you, he instantly knew who you were because you reminded him of your father. He remembered that little grandson who was given away to the monastery. You gave him peace and wisdom in that first meeting itself."

"I will now liberate you," saying this, he smeared my parched, dry lips with water.

I felt a sudden streak of light pass through my entire body. I closed my eyes. In my mind's eye the face of the young, kind monk shone like a bright, lone star.

A Mussoorie Tale

She was running as fast as her legs could carry her slight frame. To an observer it would seem as if her feet grazed the rough, hilly terrain laced with patches of rhododendrons and wild dandelions. Her eyes sparkled like that of a deer taking refuge amidst the trees in the dead of the night. Her face was flushed as she cut through the cold air. She never failed to rub a generous amount of *kohl* to add verve to an otherwise nondescript face. Her mother would apply a tiny black dot behind her ears when she left for school—a belief that it would keep her daughter safe and protect her from evil eyes. Now, they were all smudged and wet with sweat beads drawing sharp lines across her face, which was in no way becoming.

She stopped to catch her breath, her slim hands resting on her hips as she panted with quick, forceful inhales that threatened to tear her lungs apart. Perspiring profusely under her school uniform in spite of the nippy weather, she removed her sweater and tied it around her waist. She had no choice but to run away, else they would kill and feed her body parts to the jackals.

A girl born with a silver spoon and a heart of gold—what had she done that forced her to run away from home?

This is the story of Shazia Abdul Khan and me, Pia Jennifer.

******

Abdul Jehangir Khan belonged to the Balti community, originally of Tibetan descent, whose ancestors made India their home after the 1947 partition. Prior to that, Baltistan was governed by the state of Jammu and Kashmir, along with Ladakh. After partition, Baltistan came under the territory of Pakistan. However, a tiny portion was merged with Ladakh after the Indo-Pakistan war of 1971. Historically, Baltistan was a strategic point for both the countries as Kargil and Siachen wars were fought there. Over the generations, this close-knit Balti community prospered as merchants of spices, dry fruits and garments, catering mostly to the Middle Eastern countries and some parts of India. They were a tribe who honoured their religion and customs and shunned—to the point of getting violent—anything that went against the fundamentals of Islam. They abided by, *"An eye for an eye, a tooth for a tooth."* The local people knew this and their boundaries.

Shazia Abdul Khan was the only child of Abdul Jehangir Khan and his wife, Naaz. His first wife had died whilst giving birth to their fourth child. At her behest, he had taken a second wife and was happy to have been blessed with a girl child after four boys. Jehangir Khan doted on Shazia. She grew up under her mother's care. Her father was overprotective and made sure she was well guarded, not just from evil eyes but all the boys whose hormones went out of control.

"What are they called, teenage crutches or something? Make sure all that nonsense doesn't happen, *samjhe*?" father had said.

"She is no *hoorpari*," Fayaz guffawed. No lad in his right mind would as much as take a second look at our sister."

"*Shukran Allah*, our burden reduces," said Aamir raising his hands to the skies.

"What if she was a *hoorpari*? Imagine the fun we would have bashing up the boys in town," Omar remarked as he put the *hookah* to his brown lips.

"*Inshallah*, I will look after our sister, no matter what," thought Bashir but remained silent. He was not boisterous like his older brothers. He loved listening to romantic Sufi songs, poems and played the *iktara*, a one string instrument, which Siddiqui had taught him. Not anymore.

"I will not allow you to corrupt the minds of young boys and girls," Jehangir Khan had roared and ousted Siddiqui from entering the precincts of the town. Shazia and Bashir felt the absence of their beloved Sufi uncle more than anyone else.

"Who was to know that she had stolen his book of poems and stashed it under her mattress?"

"Who was to know that it would stir up a hornet's nest?"

******

The Mercedes glided to a halt at the entrance of the prestigious private school in Mussoorie, a dainty hill-station nestled in the foothills of the Himalayas. During the colonial era, International schools were set up for the British children in such cosy hill-stations with favourable climatic conditions. In present times, these schools catered to the rich, famous and influential.

"Nawaaz *bhai*, please stop the car a few blocks away. I want to walk with the rest of the girls," said Shazia in a soft voice which was barely a whisper. The driver smiled and the car stopped. But his eyes did not wander until he saw Shazia enter the school gate. He had to listen to the girl yet obey his master's *hukm*.

"These are no ordinary enclosures; they are nearly one hundred years old and made of wrought iron and embellished with the carving of two lions, signifying that the students will be treated like royalty and would eventually become leaders of the country," wafted the shrill voice of Raju, the guide, who stood imperiously at the gate, surrounded by a group of tourists. Nawaaz looked disapprovingly when they clicked pictures of the gate from various angles.

"This is not Buckingham Palace. I am going to report this matter," he rolled down the windows and shouted at the guide and the flabbergasted tourists, as the car swerved and gathered speed.

From inside the school, I noticed the swanky car and a frail girl with long neatly braided hair and shining black shoes, alight from the car. She was different from the rest, modest and quiet. She walked with a slouch, as if ashamed of her wealth. Even from that distance, I could see her dark eyes. They reminded me of the princess who had a thousand stories to tell, but could not speak.

******

In spite of Shazia's protests, Nawaaz would wait outside the class with her lunch box every afternoon. As the other girls moved towards the spacious lunch room, monitored by the teacher, Shazia would slip off the queue, quickly grab her box and signal him to go away. The girls giggled, envied, ignored and even pitied her lack of freedom.

"Whoever wants a bodyguard?" Boarding school is where all the mischief between boys and girls start and our school was no exception. Most of the students were away from their parents except a handful. I have seen paper arrows being thrown at girls—love notes—whom to meet, when, where and how. Not one was aimed at me, and I tried hard to keep my pride intact. My feelings went into my "basket of fucks," to be flung back when the time came. I had read about this and since then fallen in love with this ingenious idea. *"If I could save myself from being unhappy, why on earth should I not have one?"*

My lunch box was pretty standard with sandwiches and fruit. Same tomato and cheese sandwich, same salt-pepper taste and same smell. Thankfully, the fruit changed with the season, sometimes apple and many times lychee which was abundant in Dehra, a city close to Mussoorie. In fact, every single house there had lychee trees, a signature tree like the cherry blossoms in Japan.

I was the only one who waited for Shazia. We walked together towards the banyan tree, our cosy cafeteria, amidst the lush green landscape. Those eyes followed us everywhere. Creepy ... I flinched and felt sorry for my friend.

"Why doesn't he leave you out of sight? Does he think the earth will swallow you or you will vanish in the valley?" I joked.

"Oh! You mean Nawaaz?" Shazia brushed off my remark with a wave of her hand.

She never said a word about or against her family. On the contrary, I loved to talk about my family, distant uncles and aunts who were not relevant in our lives anymore. But I hardly spoke about my mother, of whom I was very possessive. Being a fatherless child, my mother played both the roles.

I was thankful to God for letting me be free-spirited and not shackled like my friend who had everything except the one most important thing, freedom. Even happiness went inside my basket, to spread the cheer when the time came.

"Are you wondering as to how I came to be at this elitist school?" My mother, Jennifer, taught English and she was the best teacher. The trustee, Mr. Becker, waived my tuition fee which made our life so much easier. "How was I to know that my mother was also his mistress?" The matter was kept under wraps that not even a fly could get a wind of their spicy, hot affair. I came to know about this much later when Shazia had run away from school and the police started investigating. That's when this secret slowly unravelled, not that it had anything to do with the running away, but when police dig deep, skeletons pop out and so they snoop around thinking that everybody's personal life is their bloody business. Since this exposé, my opinion about my mother changed. It saddened me when I came to know that I was not the only one in her life. I had believed in her so much that I never questioned about my father. My basket was now getting all fucked up.

None of this would have happened, but for that day. We were in the bathroom and I was tying my shoelaces.

"Pia, will you be my best friend?" Shazia asked.

I looked up but she didn't meet my eyes. She was looking far away at the skies, partly visible from the shutters of the window. It was clear and blue, the same colour as our uniform.

"I already am."

"Will you be my special friend?"

"Of course, but what is the difference between best and special?"

And then ...

She kissed me, fully on my lips. Her face was red and my lips were wet. This was my first kiss, ever. I felt the heat of her body against mine. I was taken aback, had not seen this coming, and that too from Shazia, modest and shy. What surprised me even more was the fact that it didn't feel gross. Not one bit, and that astonished me. At that moment, it dawned upon me why I never got love notes or a date invite. "Who would mess with the daughter of a teacher?" is what I had thought. But then I understood. My demeanour must have been a giveaway that I was different. I was unaware of it, until this moment. That kiss upset my brain cells, causing a medley of emotions—ecstasy, joy, confusion, realisation, but certainly not fright, shame or, "How was I going to tell this to my mother?"

"You are so beautiful. Look at me. We will make a pair of beauty and the beast," I heard her say. The next second I grabbed Shazia and kissed her back. We were locked in each other's arms for God knows how long. Everything came to a standstill. Then we heard the church bell which meant it was time to get back to class.

I left first and went straight to the class. Shazia was meant to follow after five minutes. I felt Nawaaz's eyes on me and looked around. He was nowhere to be seen. Maybe he had gone for a smoke or was hiding behind a bush. He freaked me out, all of a sudden. I tried to walk as jauntily as I could and turned around and yelled, "Hurry up Shazia, otherwise you are going to be late and the teacher won't let you in." No teacher had the guts to do so. All this was for the benefit of Nawaaz, just in case.

I sat at my desk as the teacher spoke avidly about Moghul history. I had more important things to think about. My mind was playing tricks. I had learnt something about myself and I was coming to terms with that. My eyes wandered to the handsome boy in class, it stirred no feelings. I looked at the most attractive girl in class. My heart fluttered.

"Pia, why are you looking around? Pay attention." The teacher's voice sounded like an echo from a distant drum. I could not focus.

"What would be my mother's reaction?" I wondered.

At that time, I had no clue about my mother's affair with Mr. Becker. Else I wouldn't have bothered about her feelings. Nevertheless, I made up my mind to stay quiet for a few days and give it some more time to make sure we felt the same way about each other. This was more serious and not something that I could toss into my basket.

The class ended and Shazia was nowhere to be seen.

"Where could she have gone?" My mind raced. But I had to sit through the remaining two classes and that too without a break. I dared not go to the bathroom for some strange reason.

That was the last I saw Shazia. Two days seemed like two years. On the third day, two men in uniform came to the class. I was afraid when I was taken in for questioning. I said nothing except that we were friends. I omitted the words, "best" or "special." They looked bloody tough and I told myself that they had to be tough to stay in the force. I decided to tell no one—not even my mother, not even my basket—about the kiss.

******

Shazia wished the dark skies would close in and take her in her arms. She was desperate. Her family would not hesitate to sacrifice her to *Allah*. Not just that, they would not spare Pia either.

This situation may seem weird in present times, especially with the gay community triggering angry protests demanding their rights, activists supporting and political parties opposing them; forcing the justice system to recognise those who are biologically unique to be accepted as part of our society, global human society.

In a country like India with staunch religious beliefs, ancient customs and traditions, where discrimination between castes still prevails and so does honour killings, it is ironical that homosexuality eventually got legal recognition.

"Does this mean that all families will understand and accept it?"

"How was the Khan family going to accept anything against the rudiments of Islam?"

******

Shazia kept running towards Sufi uncle's house. This was a name coined by her when she had started reading his songs and poems. She would read that one poem, over and over again. The verses mesmerised her:

My eyes refused to blink, lest she might vanish

Softness of her flesh, smooth and silky

Heaving of her chest, a quick rush of adrenalin

I stole a glance, our eyes met

I shut mine tight—baffled, shy, afraid

"Blasphemy," my mind cried. I ignored.

A deep breath, I inhaled the aura of jasmine

She halted, I held my breath

She embraced me tight, I quivered like a leaf

"Blasphemy," my mind cried again and again.

They were bold but she was not. She was sixteen and cooped up in a patriarchal household where nobody was allowed to express anything freely. The only time she felt free was whilst reading Sufi uncle's writings. She was caught up in emotions that were far beyond her to handle.

******

Siddiqui was adding splashes of colour to the painting, trying to escape the pain he felt from being unable to enter his town, where he was born and raised. When his own community branded him a *kafir* and kicked him and his young pregnant wife out, his grief knew no bounds. Those who had enjoyed and praised his Sufism, songs and poems, had turned against him. Just that one poem, "She," where he brought together two soul mates of the same sex, a union in both mind and body, had changed everything. That is also when he saw the dark side of the Khan family—Abdul Jehangir Khan.

There was a distinct knock at his door interrupting his thoughts. His wife was asleep. He saw through the peephole and felt paralysed. He recognised Shazia instantly.

"Why was she at his door at this hour?" She was alone and that scared him even more. "Was his life under some sort of threat? Was she bringing a *paigam?*"

"Open up, please." The faint voice from the other side wafted through the wafer-thin door that separated them. He went inside and woke his wife up. Both came out and opened the door. As soon as the girl entered, they quickly shut the door, after taking a sweeping glance outside. Pin drop stillness, both inside and outside.

The three of them sat in stony silence. Siddiqui motioned his wife to get some water. The girl drank quietly and started weeping.

"Aren't you Shazia?"

She nodded. "I admired your poems and songs so much so that …"

"So much so that?" Siddiqui became restless.

"I don't know how to say this. Sufi uncle, I am different."

Siddiqui and Shakila exchanged glances.

"Spell it out clearly. What do you mean you are different?" asked Shakila in a comforting tone.

"I kissed Pia, my best friend. I have come to seek refuge," Shazia blurted and stopped weeping.

Their jaws dropped. "What sort of a joke was this?" In the middle of the night, Abdul Jehangir Khan's daughter was confessing that she had kissed a girl. The face of Jehangir Khan and his tough young boys flashed in his mind threateningly and Siddiqui shuddered.

Shazia was just trouble, nothing else, and he wanted to throw her out. He was already an outcast. If they found that Shazia was with them, none would be spared.

She was huffing and stuttering to say something more.

They flinched.

"I am sorry for jeopardising your safety, but Sufi uncle, I didn't know where else to go."

******

It was the school principal who reported to the police that Shazia was missing. Abdul Jehangir Khan was furious and his sons went ballistic, but they dared not question the decision of the principal to alert the police. Too much was at stake. They had to find Shazia.

"I will chop off his balls!" A fuming Jehangir Khan told his sons to look for Shazia and the boy with whom she eloped, a foregone conclusion by an angry father.

******

I had no regrets. I loved it when Shazia had pressed her lips against mine. Her tongue had explored my mouth and I had shivered in rhapsody. That moment passed but since then I had been longing for more. My heart cried out for my special friend. The torment, the pain did not subside even as I tossed it in my basket.

My first love had gone missing. I was distressed to the point that I started menstruating, my first period. I remembered Shazia telling me about hers. Since then, I had been eagerly waiting to share my experience with her.

"What the fuck!"

******

And then one day, I found an envelope in my letter box. With hands trembling I ripped it open.

"Can you come here?" Shazia had scribbled an address. I knew where she was.

My "basket of fucks," had no place to hold the turmoil my mind was going through. I dared not go to her family or the police or tell my mother about it. I would have to skip school and face the wrath of my mother. I was willing to risk it. I decided to go the following day.

As I was about to knock at Sufi uncle's door, I heard their conversation.

"Why the hell did you do it?" said a male voice.

"I didn't do anything. It was really an accident. Why don't you believe me?" said the female voice.

This had to be Sufi uncle and his wife.

"I want you to look me in the eye and say that you are innocent. Swear in the name of our baby."

"What if I wasn't? I am the mother of your child and you would give me away? That girl was nothing but trouble. Why did she have to come here and drag us into all this? Is it not enough that we are outcasts, already?" His wife's angry shrill sounded ugly.

Siddiqui could not come to terms with the fact that his gentle and loving wife was a cold-blooded murderer.

"I am telling you repeatedly that I had not planned it. On impulse I pushed her in the canal, as we were taking a walk this morning. I fled after that and didn't look back. I was afraid and regretted it. I swear nobody saw us together."

My hands flew to my mouth to suppress a scream.

I knew Shazia could swim.

"Why didn't she? Had she?" I searched within for an answer. If I was her soulmate, I should know. But my mind was blank.

I took the last bus back home. My mother was waiting anxiously. I barely heard when she said that Shazia was found dead in the canal. I felt a wave of nausea and blanked out.

The death of Shazia remained a mystery in Mussoorie, except for me.

******

Nestled under the warmth of our favourite banyan tree, I wrote:

Her gait was unsteady but her mind was filled with courage and resolve. She didn't have the faintest idea where she was headed. The street was deserted. What else would you expect at the dead of night? She was unafraid of the dark but fearful of the shadows that were following her. She halted. They were now an ugly clump ahead of her, moving zigzag like a bloody maniac. She took a deep breath and started walking. The clump started moving faster and faster, disappearing in the wilderness. She took another deep breath and smiled.

"What was she chasing?"

It was the beacon of hope. Yes! She was chasing hope when life was closing in on her. She had to leave behind those dark shadows that taunted her. She had to grab the last rays of hope and embrace them wholeheartedly. Have utmost faith that only she can fight for the lovely life God had bestowed upon her and was now threatening to tear to shreds. Her body was growing tired but her mind was alert. It was her best ally that was prompting her to go beyond the vast expanse of darkness, towards the shimmering light at the end of a dark tunnel.

"Hope, Faith, Courage; Hope, Faith, Courage; Hope, Faith, Courage ..." She smiled and her gait became steady. Her footsteps made a soft sound that nobody could hear, except her.

"Will she get a new leash of life?"

"Will she get another chance to recreate her life?"

"I will blow soap bubbles and build sandcastles on the beach. I will do all the silly things as if the world was made just for me. I will use my strength and knowledge to help others, less fortunate. I will ... I will ... I will ..."

She heard footsteps. The street was not deserted anymore. It was not dark anymore. The sky was luminous with a tinge of reddish orange as dawn broke out. Several people had joined her as they all headed towards the beacon.

"Hope, Faith, Courage; Hope, Faith, Courage; Hope, Faith, Courage ..." reverberated in the air and mingled with the dew drops.

I closed my eyes thinking of Shazia. If only she had the courage, if only she had not lost hope, if only she had ...

******

Glossary

Bhai	*Brother*
Hoorpari	*Stunning angel*
Hukm	*Command*
Hookah	*Oriental tobacco pipe*
Inshallah	*God willing*
Kafir	*Who defies the principles of Islam*
Kohl	*Black powder used as eye makeup*
Paigam	*Message*
Samjhe	*Do you understand?*
Shukran Allah	*Thank God*

About the Author

Ms. Revathi Raj Iyer is the author of two books—"My Friendship with Yoga," and "Syra's Secret—Diverse Short Stories from Siliguri, Singapore and beyond." She is also an editor, beta reader, book reviewer and yoga/fitness enthusiast. Professionally qualified in Law and Company/Chartered Secretary from India and New Zealand, Revathi has worked in a multinational and also as lecturer of Laws. After returning from Fiji, a spiritual enrichment break inspired her to write. Her stories, poems, book reviews and articles have been published both in print and online media. She enjoys writing short stories as she believes that fiction gives a chance to express and recreate life. She lives in the vibrant city of Ahmedabad, India, with her husband and continues to write enchanting stories.

My Friendship with Yoga
Photo credit: Lifi Publications

Syra's Secret—Diverse Short Stories
Photo credit: Become Shakespeare

www.ingramcontent.com/pod-product-compliance
Lightning Source LLC
LaVergne TN
LVHW041558070526
838199LV00046B/2039